Dear Parents and Educators,

Welcome to Penguin Young Readers! As parents and educators, you know that each child develops at his or her own pace—in terms of speech, critical thinking, and, of course, reading. Penguin Young Readers recognizes this fact. As a result, each Penguin Young Readers book is assigned a traditional easy-to-read level (1–4) as well as a Guided Reading Level (A–P). Both of these systems will help you choose the right book for your child. Please refer to the back of each book for specific leveling information. Penguin Young Readers features esteemed authors and illustrators, stories about favorite characters, fascinating nonfiction, and more!

Cork & Fuzz: Wait a Minute

LEVEL **3**

GUIDED
READING
LEVEL **J**

This book is perfect for a **Transitional Reader** who:
- can read multisyllable and compound words;
- can read words with prefixes and suffixes;
- is able to identify story elements (beginning, middle, end, plot, setting, characters, problem, solution); and
- can understand different points of view.

Here are some **activities** you can do during and after reading this book:
- Make Predictions: At the end of the story, Cork and Fuzz bury the sun seed so that it will grow into a sun flower. How long do you think they will wait for it to grow? What will Cork and Fuzz do to help the sun seed grow? Do you think the sun seed will grow into a flower? What will happen?
- Make Connections: Cork is good at waiting, but Fuzz hates to wait. Have you ever had to wait for something? What did you wait for? What did it feel like? Was it worth the wait in the end?

Remember, sharing the love of reading with a child is the best gift you can give!

—Bonnie Bader, EdM
  Penguin Young Readers program

*Penguin Young Readers are leveled by independent reviewers applying the standards developed by Irene Fountas and Gay Su Pinnell in *Matching Books to Readers: Using Leveled Books in Guided Reading*, Heinemann, 1999.

For Katrina, Evan, and Aleah—DC

To Amy, friends forever!—LM

PENGUIN YOUNG READERS
Published by the Penguin Group
Penguin Group (USA) LLC, 375 Hudson Street, New York, New York 10014, USA

USA | Canada | UK | Ireland | Australia | New Zealand | India | South Africa | China

penguin.com
A Penguin Random House Company

The original art was created using scratchboard, pen and ink, and watercolor.

Text copyright © 2014 by Dori Chaconas. Illustrations copyright © 2014 by Lisa McCue.
All rights reserved. Previously published in hardcover in 2014 by Penguin Young Readers.
This paperback edition published in 2015 by Penguin Young Readers, an imprint of
Penguin Group (USA) LLC, 345 Hudson Street, New York, New York 10014. Manufactured in China.

Library of Congress Control Number: 2013013069

ISBN 978-0-14-750856-0   10 9 8 7 6 5 4 3 2 1

PENGUIN YOUNG READERS

LEVEL 3

TRANSITIONAL READER

CORK & FUZZ

Wait a Minute

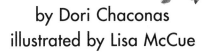

by Dori Chaconas

illustrated by Lisa McCue

Penguin Young Readers
An Imprint of Penguin Group (USA) LLC

Chapter 1

Cork was a short muskrat.

He knew how to wait.

If he was cold in winter, he said,

"Oh well, I will wait for spring."

If he was hungry, he said,

"Oh well, I will wait for lunch."

If Fuzz slept late, Cork said,

"Oh well, I will wait for him to

wake up."

Fuzz was a tall possum.

He did not like to wait.

If he was cold in winter, he said,

"Oh, nuts! I want it to be

spring now!"

If he was hungry, he said,

"Oh, nuts! I want lunch now!"

If Cork slept late, Fuzz said,

"Cork, wake up!

Wake up right now!"

Two best friends.

One knew how to wait.

The other one just knew how

to be Fuzz.

One day Cork sat on a stump

in Fuzz's yard.

"We can play Follow the Leader,"

Fuzz said.

"I will be the leader."

He hopped on one foot.

"Wait a minute," Cork said,

looking up at the sky.

"I do not want to wait," Fuzz said.

He hopped on the other foot.

Cork did not hop.

He was still looking up.

"Wait a minute," he said again.

"I do not want to wait," Fuzz said.

He stamped his foot.

"You are not following the leader!"

"Wait a minute!" Cork said.

He pointed up.

"Look!"

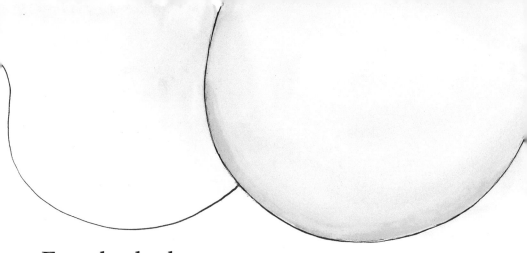

Fuzz looked up.

Something big and round
and yellow floated above them.

"What is that?" Cork asked.

"The sun!" Fuzz yelled.

"The sun is falling!
Run!"

Chapter 2

"Wait a minute!" Cork said.

But Fuzz was already hiding under

a pokeberry bush.

Cork crawled in after him.

"Why are you hiding?" Cork asked.

Fuzz said,

"Because the sun is falling.

The sun will fall on our heads!"

Cork said, "I do not think it is the sun.

The sun is over there."

"Then what is it?" Fuzz asked.

"It is big and round and yellow

like the sun."

Cork said, "Maybe the sun

laid an egg.

Maybe it is a sun egg."

"An egg?" Fuzz asked.

He crawled out from under the bush.

"I am not afraid of an egg.

We can catch it!

We can hatch it!"

"Wait for me!" Cork said.

The wind pushed the sun egg toward
the top of a hill.

Fuzz ran up the hill.

Zoom! Zoom! Zoom!

Cork ran up the hill, too.

Wump! Wump!

The wind changed.

The sun egg floated toward the

bottom of the hill.

Fuzz ran down the hill.

Zoom! Zoom! Zoom!

Cork ran down the hill, too.

Wump! Wump!

The sun egg caught on the top
of a tree.

A very, very tall tree.

"Now what do we do?" Cork asked.

"We climb the tree," Fuzz said.

"We catch the sun egg.

Then we hatch it."

"Wait!" Cork said.

"We cannot climb this tree.

It is too big.

Maybe we can blow it down."

Cork blew.

Poof! Poof!

Nothing happened.

"Maybe we can shake it down."

Cork pushed on the tree trunk.

Oof! Oof!

Nothing happened.

"Maybe we can kick it down."

Cork kicked the tree trunk.

"Owwww!"

"Oh, nuts!" Fuzz said.

"I cannot wait any longer."

Chapter 3

Fuzz climbed up the tree.

He climbed into the leaves until

Cork could no longer see him.

Cork waited.

"Did you catch the egg yet?"

he called up into the tree.

"No," Fuzz said.

Cork waited some more.

"Did you catch the egg yet?"

he called again.

"No," Fuzz said.

Cork waited longer.

"Did you catch the egg yet?"

he called once more.

"Oh, nuts!" Fuzz said.

"What is the matter?" Cork yelled.

"There is a tweeter bird up here,"
Fuzz answered.

"He is trying to peck my head."

Tweet!

"Ouch!"

Just then the wind blew

the sun egg free.

"Fuzz," Cork yelled, "come down!

The egg is unstuck.

It is floating toward my pond."

"Wait for me!" Fuzz yelled.

Cork and Fuzz ran to the pond.

Zoom! Zoom! Zoom!

Wump! Wump!

"OWWWW!"

Fuzz banged his toe on a rock.

He tumbled to the pond bank.

"The egg is floating on the pond,"
Cork said.

"We can catch it."

"No, wait!" Fuzz yelled.

"I cannot swim!"

"Yes, you can swim," Cork said.

"You know how to kick and paddle."

"I cannot kick and paddle because my toe hurts!" Fuzz said.

"Then wait here," Cork said.

"I will catch it."

"No, no, no!" Fuzz said.

"I do not want to wait!"

Cork scratched his head.

"Hold my tail," he said.

"I will pull you.

We will catch the egg together."

Chapter 4

Fuzz grabbed Cork's tail.

Cork swam toward the sun egg.

"Ouch!" Fuzz yelled.

"Does your toe hurt?" Cork asked.

"No," said Fuzz.

"My tail hurts!

Something is biting it!

OUCH!"

Cork grabbed the sun egg.

"I got it!" he yelled.

He swam back to the pond bank.

Cork climbed out of the pond with
Fuzz on his tail.

Fuzz climbed out of the pond with
a crayfish on his tail.

"Get it off me!" Fuzz yelled.

Fuzz flipped his tail.

The crayfish flipped up into the air.

Then the crayfish grabbed

the sun egg.

POP!

Cork blinked at Fuzz.

Fuzz blinked at Cork.

They both blinked at the popped

yellow thing.

"It is not an egg after all," Cork said.

"Then what is it?" Fuzz asked.

"Maybe it is a sun seed," Cork said.

"We can plant it.

Maybe a sun flower will grow."

And so they did.

Two best friends dug a hole.

They planted the sun seed.

Then they sat and watched

and waited for something beautiful

to grow.

"Do we have to wait long?"

Fuzz asked.

"Maybe," said Cork.

"Nuts!" said Fuzz.